# About the Author

Ella has worked in a variety of roles, from academic lecturing to TV presenting. In the corporate world her focus was originally in sales and marketing, working with internationals in brand management, and more recently in business coaching and personal development.

After graduating from St. John's Oxford in Philosophy & Theology she attained MCIM and then pursued a range of stress management qualifications. One of the techniques she uses with clients is to help them to write, or to re-write, their 'story', and this has now become the basis for 'Silicon Tales' – a collection of modern fairytales that help the reader to explore some of life's challenges and changes, in a creative, succinct and impactful way.

Ella's passion is to promote 'self help' to those who are most scathing about it. So was she. But now she's as likely to be seen writing a story in a canal side pub in Warwickshire as she is to be seen suited in a city meeting.

# Silicon Tales

## Story-telling for the Digital Age

# SILICON
# TALES

ELLA PRICE

SilverWood

Published in 2013 by the author using
SilverWood Books Empowered Publishing®

SilverWood Books
30 Queen Charlotte Street, Bristol BS1 4HJ
www.silverwoodbooks.co.uk

This is a work of fiction. Names, characters, places and incidents either are
products of the author's imagination or are used fictitiously. Any resemblance
to actual events or locales or persons, living or dead, is entirely coincidental.

ISBN 978-1-78132-072-3 (paperback)
ISBN 978-1-78132-073-0 (ebook)

British Library Cataloguing in Publication Data
A CIP catalogue record for this book is available from the British Library

Set in Sabon by SilverWood Books
Printed on paper sourced responsibly

*For those who dare to tell*

# Contents

# A Word from the Author

Thank you for choosing this book. I know, from personal experience, that the idea of 'adult fairytales' can raise all sorts of ridicule and hackles. It's a bit like being offered the Wii controls when you're 43 at a cool teenage party and feeling as familiar with virtual wakeboarding as you are with the surface of Mars.

Anyway, thank you for getting over that.

This book was inspired by the challenge: if your life story were to be told as a fairytale, what might happen after 'Once upon a time…'?

My story is not included here. Sorry – maybe in a future edition. Nor are any of my client's stories included or even hinted at, although many have found this approach surprisingly useful.

This is just a collection of stories that have cropped up along the way, often when I was hardly even thinking of a 'story' but then out one popped, prompted by anything from the most mundane of experiences to the rather more profound. I don't honestly know why they exist. But I suspect that you may.

Do take a view on the Fright, Fight, Flight sections; it might be best to dip into one section at a time dependent on your mood, or do feel free to skip a whole section altogether if they're really not for you. And unless you fancy a sleepless night, I'd suggest that you don't read from cover-to-cover. Please don't overload your chip!

I'd like you to enjoy these tales – in whichever way you like. There are layers to them and you might read a story and find something in it that no one else does. I'd like to think they're a bit like pop songs – fleeting bits of words and rhythm you might click with for a few minutes, but occasionally one might strike such a chord that you hum it for a while after.

And the reason for your humming will be yours alone.

Storytelling is a tool that's often claimed as a novel discovery in the therapy industry. It isn't. From aeons past, the campfire or clan gatherings encouraged this simple art, which is now a little lost with all the complex gadgets and gizmos of a digital age.

But you write your own story everyday. In every choice you make. So telling it in a modern 'fairytale' way can help you to take a different look at it.

And maybe even re-write it.

If you would like to share your story with me and perhaps feature in a future edition, please do so via www.silicontales.com.

Because 43 year olds have been known to be virtual wakeboarding champions at the very first play, you know...

Ella Price

December 2012

# For the FIGHT

*Tales to tussle over, with room for your own interpretation...*

# The Special Coil of Chemicals

Once upon a time there was a special coil of chemicals. And this special coil of chemicals had lain hidden for very many centuries. In fact, it's likely it had remained hidden from the beginning of time itself. But then aeons later, in 1869 or thereabouts, it was discovered by some very clever boffins to just happen to contain within it the very building blocks of just about everything. Well, everything that really mattered anyway. Like babies and chameleons and Labrador dogs and pansies.

It was a double helix of life itself, a coil of creation with a bar code potential for swiping every twist and turn of every living thing you could possibly imagine into the hyper market of this hyper varied world.

Yowzer.

For such, it seems, is the importance of patterns: from knitting balaclavas, to military invasions, to a course of psychotherapy. Patterns, patterns, patterns...knit 1, nuke 1, know 1...it all starts with a basic pattern scribbled on the back of an envelope somewhere. A pattern, which to anyone who has not the eyes to see might just be a doodle of gobbledegook, but to those who are in the know, it's the glowing golden key to unlock all knowledge.

And so, like apples on a tree that we're told we're not allowed to eat from, well, we just have to, don't we?

Yes, this special coil of chemicals, this twist on life itself, once discovered then could not be undiscovered. A bit like the discovery of adultery: it's where the trust really has to start. Oh, the responsibility! Because to know even a wee smidgen of this special coil of chemical's twisty turns meant that you could conjure up a chameleon that dutifully yapped and wagged its tale and fetched your newspaper, or pansy petals that grew teeth and bawled and cried out for a mother's milk.

Such was the responsibility of making its acquaintance.

As an aside to my story – or perhaps it is the story itself – I've heard it said that knowledge is power, and that power corrupts. As if this is an absolute ancient truth, inevitable and irresistible. Well, perhaps it is. But to me it isn't clear if the corruption is of the knower or of the knowledge itself.

Let's see...

Perhaps only the end of our story will tell.

For indeed, there had been many stories in aeons past of Gods in glorious parts of the known and unknown world who dabbled with such things. Oh, it may not have been called 'genetics', but ancient tales of mermaids with siren voices or donkey heads on dumb ass characters in a Shakespeare play amount to much the same thing – blends and boggling mixes of the basic building blocks of life. Avatars throughout the ages bear witness to my claim.

Yes, in its day this special coil of chemicals had twisted its helix in many a mutation for the sake of mysticism or entertainment of the masses. It had been debated over many crates of beers, and its daring potential had been used to frighten hordes of small children for centuries, and all the time it had never been named: until 1869. Clever little coil – very twisty indeed!

Until...one fateful day, the spark of a new idea hit it with full force, bowling at it like a wild giant hurricane from the hands of master technicians who hoped to purify it and concentrate it into an absolute pattern, a perfect blueprint, to be cloned whenever the world (or Herr und Frau Schmidt) needed a God to be born. A Godling of the purest double loop, a genetic dream, a Man-god walking among us to rival all the faulty Gods of the ancient world, with their various pyrrhic victories and Achilles heels.

Perhaps, even, a God-man to rival the gods themselves.

Now – you see, we designed to design our own tree.

But, fortunately for the modern world, loops are extremely aptly named. They are rather full of themselves, in the very nicest kind of way.

Perfection and stability certainly aren't core in-bred qualities of loops and coils. Let me ask you, have you ever tried drinking a cocktail on a bobbing wave? Perfection and stability might be the very fleeting fluke moments that the straw actually makes it into your mouth and not into your eye – a happy circumstance, a lucky draw, but often a misnomer anyway.

That depends on the cocktail.

Because this special coil of chemicals had a habit that it just couldn't break: of twisting, often in imperceptibly small ways. Such that whatever may have looked like a clone turned out to have some unexpected kink in it far, or sometimes not so far, down the line. I'm told that if you distil whiskey too purely, it can suddenly and unexpectedly turn into a cup of tea.

I do not propose attempting to prove that claim.

This, then, seems to be the alchemy that eludes us: the full fakery of perfection.

Thank the Gods.

Because perfection can't be static in a world made up of change – even death struggles with that absolute and ancient truth.

And therein lies the lovely loophole.

So, this special coil of chemicals,
after twisting its tale to me, and leaving
some bits out I'm sure, as was its way, went off merrily weaving
its own DNA way.

To live loopily ever after.

Somehow.

Someway.

## The Man Who Just Couldn't Bear to Wear Shoes

Once upon a time there was a man who just couldn't bear to wear shoes. He'd felt like this all his life: from a wee lad, wandering barefoot on pokey pebbles or gravelly pavements without a care, to being the kind of youth who mainly wanted to hang out at the beach, or only at venues where bare toes were cool.

But there weren't very many of those places, the wee lad realised, as he gradually and somewhat reluctantly grew up.

In fact, as time went on, he began to see how difficult it was going to be to live the life that he wanted to live. It was a pretty simple request, but he quickly learnt that slipping your shoes off on most work shifts or practically anytime at all when you were wearing a suit, even in your own home, somehow was more frowned upon than a serious drug habit or a tendency to mental cruelty.

Strange how the world's etiquette works.

Anyway, after realising that making a life's work of traditional grape-stomping was forlorn, and that even surfer dudes can get stuck in their flip flops, he found a job that let him fly a great deal – mostly long haul, and mostly alone.

So he'd be the man who you might just have spotted out

of the corner of your eye one day when you were meant to be watching the air hostess point out your escape routes and the paltry top-up device on your life jacket. He'd be the passenger breathing a huge sigh of relief and of deep release as he slipped off his shoes, hooked his big toes into the top of his socks and in one swift, clearly well-practised move, got naked under the seat of the unsuspecting passenger in front of him. He'd be the one passenger relishing the prospect of the long haul, with its total freedom from the ankle down for hours – as much as others would certainly be dreading its locked-in captive feeling and couldn't wish it done fast enough.

At such times it was as if the man who just couldn't bear to wear shoes had opened his own escape hatch and slid down the inflatable slide, squealing.

One day when he was extra long-hauling and already a few hours ankle down naked and free, his delight was abruptly interrupted by the innocent question:

'Why have you got your shoes off?' from a wee lad next to him who had a look of a kid he might have known from somewhere.

'Shhh....' said the wee lad's mother, from the window seat, restraining her son and flashing a swift look of apology to the man who just couldn't bear to wear shoes. And that look had a hint of 'I'd love to know too' and also perhaps a nervous dash of 'It's nothing catching is it?'

'If you really want to know,' said the man who couldn't bear to wear shoes, in a style that showed he was baiting them both a little, and also deeply enjoying it.

'...I love to feel the earth breathe beneath my feet. I can feel its rhythm in a way that makes my heart beat differently, and to put shoes between me and it feels like I'm suffocating'.

He surprised himself with the force with which he spoke and the tears that welled in his eyes. For perhaps he'd never said anything like this so plainly before. Or perhaps he'd never been so plainly asked.

Now the child, who had none of the embarrassment of his mother who was all of a sudden finding the cloud formations fake fascinating, turned to him.

'But we're in the air. Your feet aren't touching the earth at all...' he queried, puzzled, pointing out the obvious that yet another adult had missed.

'But can't you feel it?' said the man, whispering conspiratorially, for effect.

'What?' whispered the wee lad back, wide-eyed and utterly hooked.

'Your feet dancing in the air...it's like swimming, but also it feels like you're a bird, and a leaf, and a balloon and a high flying kite – all at once!'

And the wee lad gasped, as he did truly feel it, and he immediately dropped and fidgeted under his seat so that his mother couldn't possibly step in, as she usually did, to stop the delight he could almost taste.

A small shoe flew up and landed back in his seat. Then followed a sock, and then a growl that became a squeal...

'What have you done to my son?' said the mother, with a smile that might have said 'I wish you'd been his father' if just a smile could say such things.

'I'm not sure, but I suspect you'll be saving a lot on shoe bills from now on!' laughed the man who just couldn't bear to wear shoes.

And next to him the wee lad swept the debris of his shoes and socks off his seat and sat back and belted up and wiggled his toes on top of his fold-down tray to get them up as high in the air as possible, so that he felt like a firework exploding…and then he was all wrapped up in popping candyfloss…and then he was an astronaut, superman, a shooting star, a rocket trail…

At least, that's what he told me it felt like when we slept together years later.

More years later, the first man who just couldn't bear to wear shoes was grounded. Because he had flown so much away from this world with the etiquette that had stopped him living how he wanted to, that one day his heart beat stopped. It had just taken far too much pressure, according to the doctors. So it had to spasm very hard to make him stop escaping, and get him early-retired. No more long-haul or secret naked ankle trips. No more future, so he thought.

But the irony was, he'd almost forgotten the rhythm of the earth's heartbeat and the delight of pokey pebbles and sand-between-the-toes walks. He'd forgotten that being earth-bound actually didn't mean suffocating at all if maybe the memory of a barefoot wee lad flitted across your mind every now and again in your retirement years.

And, to the relief of all concerned, his heart began to beat differently again.

# The Tiny Nipping Bug

Once upon a time there was a tiny nipping bug. Now it wasn't a mosquito, and it wasn't a flea. Frankly, it wasn't that well known. It was really quite rare you see, and only popped into lively existence for a very few special days of the year. For the rest of its time it hung in a strange suspended animation, an insignificant speck of dust on a mirror's edge for anyone astute enough to peer at whilst picking at their teeth.

But no one ever did.

And so the tiny nipping bug came out to play year after year, effectively for a spasm of a lifetime, causing mayhem and temporary madness in all the sweet living flesh it landed on. Because cleverly, it made no sound at all; it didn't buzz, it didn't click or whistle. So perhaps what some poor person thought was a hair brushing their leg, actually turned out to be the silent poisoned pincers of the tiny nipping bug, searing a line of red hot sores that once sown would take weeks to heal and leave a nasty scar as a flashing reminder not to risk those skimpy shorts again.

In this way the tiny nipping bug, although of course it didn't know it, played its part in things as grave as the mental paranoia and panic of 'I daren't.... what if...what's that?' which is more than enough to ruin anyone's hard-fought-for fortnight in the sunshine. Because its power was that nothing could take a potshot at it. Of course, if you turn up at your holiday home and find a tiger in your kitchen, well, you go out and buy a shotgun. But a stealth bomber you can't see? At best, a flailing tea towel would be winged in desperation, or a cloud of choking repellent spray mushroomed in the air – both always, of course, miles away from where the tiny nipping bug was curiously watching. What a funny display!

Now, it might take some believing, as anyone who may have fallen prey to this tiny nipping bug or one of its equally stealthy relatives, cannot help but assert that they are evil, the devil's spawn, a vile blight on the places of this earth that are closest to paradise. That's a very understandable view when you've spent the previous fifty weeks in a concrete tower staring at a screen of data, and the two weeks of heaven you've dreamt of have turned into a scratching, itching hell.

But no such view is true.

The particular tiny nipping bug that I had a few words with after several nights of it feasting on my feet in my own planned-for paradise was frankly a delightful little chap. Honestly! I spotted him just as he came to rest on a lampshade, and while he was briefly backlit, I took a blistering swipe, as hard and as fast as I vengefully could.

'Why?' he squealed out, with a terror I could not ignore – as it echoed my very own.

'Well, I might return the question!' I snapped, scratching my ankles until they bled. Yet again.

'Because you're delicious!' he said, incredulous, as if this was the way it should be and that it was my fault for being so.

'Oh...' I lamely responded. I do admit I was rather

flummoxed by his flattery, and his words at all for that matter, '...but that doesn't give you the right to hurt me!'

'How am I hurting you?' he asked, in such an innocent, honest voice that he now became the irresistible one.

And in a bid to distract him from my ankles and armpits, and feeling not less than a little silly and definitely doubting the wisdom of that last drink, I endeavoured to explain my hurt to the tiny nipping bug.

After my efforts at an explanation, which mostly stopped him moving at least, he understood a little more, I think. Then he told me his story, and the world turned a little on its axis – although that may have been that last drink, or the first stages of blood poisoning setting in...

As a very tiny nipping bug, his mother – who was apparently legendary in the premium nipping league by all accounts – had trained him very well. There was pride and an honour as he spoke. She had military blood (probably sucked from a soldier) and her mantra was 'Get in and get out,' with an ethic of causing minimal damage and just taking enough to fuel the liveliness of the next few days. 'Enough and no more,' she'd say. Yes, her Golden Rule of bug survival was: take too much and you'll get crushed, as the heavier the speck of bug, the slower it would be to flit and the bigger it would be to spot.

Simple.

My tiny nipping bug had trained hard, being his mother's only bug. He so wanted to please her for the times they were lucky enough to share. Some years she would nudge him off the bathroom mirror frame, sometimes he would shake her awake, but they always managed to share their lively days together. Until she wasn't there one day and he had to assume the bathroom mirror owner had been rather more particular with the cleaning cloth than in previous years or lifetimes.

Do you know, I could almost picture her by this point in his story. She was, in my mind's eye, no evil harridan, no nipping witch, just a worried mother – yes, admittedly a slightly military one but a mother nonetheless – who wanted her boy to survive the cleaning cloths and tea towels of this world. Strange, the common ground of species, when you think about it.

And I could see the following scenes too...

He talked of a time when, in fear of her baby being plagued with red welts, another mother had kept her perfect girl indoors, away from the swimming pool, and coincidentally away from the prowling hands of someone who'd been waiting all day for an opportunity to steal her. And I could see the estranged couple who were forced indoors by cluster bombs of his blisters all over their distant rigid bodies, but who in being forced to nurse each other under the safe but small enclosure of a netted bed, then talked and touched and then made relaxed but careful love to each other as had only happened many years before. And I could see the would-be writer who'd told her publisher that she'd be finished after two weeks away, but who secretly knew that the lure of exploring abroad would mean that the boring book edit was relegated, again. But with badly blistered ankles, what else could she do but meet her deadline and finally nail the dream and destiny she'd been putting off all her lifetime?

It was odd how sad I was when his voice stopped.

Odder still when I tried to coax my little bug awake with a rotting apricot.

And then even with my rotting ankles.

But nothing worked. He simply hadn't taken enough.

And, as is the way with tiny nipping bugs, by morning our exchange was just a vague itching memory anyway – albeit one that wouldn't go away.

Because I have the scars to prove it.

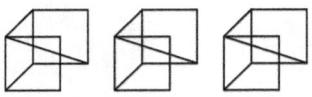

# The Power of a Promise Pledged

Once upon a time there was the binding power of a promise pledged. Now, it wasn't a specific promise, as these are made every day, often unthinkingly, in the 'I promise I will, yes honestly, if you'll just stop nagging me and get out of my face' kind of way.

We've all made these kinds of promises – not worth their weight in sock fluff.

No, we're talking about the kind of pledge that may even go unspoken, and may even not be between two people at all.

Ah yes, these are very special promises indeed.

Because sometimes they may go unnoticed totally by the very people who are pledging them, or who are being pledged to. They can indeed hang in the energy of a whole lifetime with an aura all of their own, that no one can really see with this lifetime's eyes. Oddly, least of all those involved. Until maybe, just possibly generations later, when a family tree gets drawn up sometime, and a cute great-granddaughter might realise 'That must have been the pledge he made!' as the reason why great-granddad died as a wealthy youth or maybe lived to 104, penniless.

These sorts of pledges can pan out either way.

The point is, they are always powerful, often imperceptible and make the word 'pledge' sound frankly far too light and cosy. Life oaths they are, with consequences grave.

It was decided one day by the Oath Committee (of these things I really shouldn't say too much) that one of these powerfully pledged promises was getting a bit too big for its boots. Actually, if it had owned a pair of boots it would probably have given them away to the poor. That was the heart of the problem...

Because the oath the Committee was considering for nullification (a process they'd made up, of course, but committees do excel at that) was an instance that they had seen well-evidenced of late in a young lad, maybe aged only seven or eight. He had a phenomenal talent with a tennis ball in his back yard which, when he got the chance to put his footwork into practice on the football field was utterly breathtaking and potentially monumental. But for some reason he would suddenly choose to play the idiot, the loser, even the fumbler. Particularly when the talent scouts were on the touchlines and especially if his parents were anywhere near.

The reason for his choice was that his elder brother, who wasn't anywhere near as gifted, and was wheezy and cry-baby and frankly embarrassingly clingy, might be judged less pathetic by his parents in this life.

Because his brother had chosen to be less in his life too.

Now that's a pledge oft-spoken, oft-unseen, a powerful life oath with consequences grave indeed.

And the Committee had seen this oath's influence far too often: in wives, in children, in sons, husbands and even soldiers – in fact, in all the places where an oath to have a shining life would have been the right decision, but an oath *not* to, was judged to be even better.

Oh dear. How could the dusty Committee (if you knew where they were based, you'd understand), how could they affect the power of this pledge and 'de-attractify' it? You can tell, they discussed this at such length that a whole vocabulary developed.

On this occasion a new Committee member, an intern, not long sworn in and still technically on probation (as membership was eternal and risks really could not be taken) piped up – which in itself broke a little of the power of the 'let's not shine' delusional pledge. This irony was not lost on the Committee, senile as most were.

'What if we use another oath to 'nullify' the profound attraction of this one?'

The intern was aeons younger than the next youngest member, but she was smart and she was brave and she knew she had to talk the talk in order to stand a chance of the Committee hearing her, let alone them drawing up a rightly worded resolution and despite the ages that it would take them to ratify it – oh, the power games committees play!

'What about the special pledge of "I'll never lose sight of myself"?' she ploughed on, as she could see that she'd managed to wake at least half of the other members from their slumbers or senility.

'Not strong enough!' yawned and groaned a dinosaur, but also a darkly astute member who wasn't quite a fossil yet.

'You can pledge to remember, but sacrifice yourself still.' And he extinguished her bright spark with a roll of his pinhole eyes, and a flicking lick of his flaking lips that by any interpretation was downright creepy.

'Ah…' She re-arranged her seat on the bench, hard granite rock as it was, and retrieved a small family photo of her even younger self as an obese barrel of a child at a wedding when she was maybe eleven. She knew now that she had silently pledged to be so rotund and fat that she would hide her burgeoning early womanhood and not rival her mother for her father's affections. Because a sad, fat little girl stays immune from such judgements, doesn't she?

'What about, "I'll be true to who I truly am"?' she proffered.

'Fat chance!' snapped the T-Rex of a Chair, unknowingly hitting the intern's nerve.

'How often do we know who we *truly* are? Maybe yoga teachers and revolutionaries, and then, only sometimes...' He laughed a gurgling croak of ridicule. Then hacked and spat something black that hissed and steamed as it hit the ice cold floor and gave off a rotting stench.

'Point taken...' She withdrew, feeling pinched. Indeed, she felt at that moment the powerful pull of the pledge's attraction *not* to shine, to be less than she could be, to give up the fight, to let others have their day, and way, and say, to let them glory, to let them win...

After all, perhaps it wasn't that important to her anyway, and she did know her place, didn't she?

But then, without the warning of a proposal and submission that's usually needed in such settings, something welled from deep within her that was nothing short of an explosion, a roar. She managed to hide it as suppressed wind for a while (a lot of that got overlooked in the Committee room) but then it blew, irrepressibly, threatening the vaulted roof miles above...

And she stood up.

'This oath's power is surely "nullified" by the pull of the

most powerful pledge of all: to be fully human. For to be human is to evolve and progress, and this pledge is fundamentally *in*humane!'

She nearly hiccupped in shock then, wide, wet-eyed, as if her roar needed to be dialled down after the event and rebottled. But once it was out, she couldn't take it back. Instead she eyeballed each dinosaur in turn and coughed and breathed in a way that might be taken as another roar in the making. And because she felt that if she didn't, clouds of smoke would come out of her ears anyway.

She got mutters back. Fluttering mumbles that said the Committee was unsettled. Disturbed even, perhaps feeling their imminent extinction by such a bright spark?

Just as they started to expect her to generate some cosmic collision that might threaten to upset their established order forever, or maybe just to smack them all in the teeth with the back of her clenching and unclenching hand, she turned, weirdly calm and controlled, and walked out from the Committee's secret chamber. She let the ancient doors slam behind her deep in the cavern, before anyone could even start discussing a procedure in these most irregular of circumstances.

Because arguing her case with the Oath Committee was utterly irrelevant now.

For her, the oath was dead.

And the cavern was its grave.

She knew in that instant that each person who had chosen this oath at some point in their lives had to fight their own battle with it. No committee nullification could possibly help.

Because the power of this promise pledged could not be counteracted by just replacing it with another oath. It had to be seen in the cold light of a life-critical day for its appalling betrayal of the very core of human existence – the oath to end all oaths, it might be said.

And when spotted in a lifetime,  this insight could then birth the hope that the brightest spark of a person's light might just shine on.

And on.

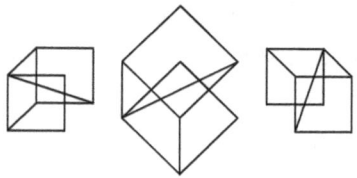

# The Gnarled Old Willow Tree

Once upon a time there was a gnarled old willow tree. This was the kind of tree that whispered 'secret ancient aeons passed' to anyone who walked by it. For twisted and almost deformed it was, in such an impressive way that it might even have taken centuries to reach such a perfect state of spookiness.

Yes, many a child had seen a fairy or a pixie peering from between its knotted branches, and many an adult had 'don't be silly' hurried them along, thinking just the same.

Ancient it was, and as with all ancient things, there is wisdom. And often there is far more kindness than wizened and gnarled things can easily show. So the gnarled old willow tree had, in truth, expended years of concentrated effort to protrude some of its very best branches down even to touch the ground, so that brave youngsters (and some not so brave or young) could make their way up into its very core. And at some wonderful point, all these brave souls would have to hug its trunk to hold their balance, as they generally climbed up at full pelt without thinking. The gnarled old willow tree loved those times with all its ancient secret heart most of all. Because it took a lifetime of focus to grow a crooked branch that might safely cradle a child; but a child could cradle its trunk in an unthinking joyous instant, pat it and pick at it and squeeze and squeal a grateful goodbye.

So moments of sheer delight were exchanged for ages of intense and focused effort.

But let me tell you the real secret of the story that the gnarled old willow tree shared: it is that the echo of that child's energy might just mean a new shoot would sprout up overnight, or the slightest cell realignment would shift a branch to exactly the right angle for another little one to fully feel its embrace – and lift their feet off the ground and swing in delight.

Such is the power of sheer joy.

And the gnarled old willow tree would have gasped at these miniscule yet magnificent changes – if trees could gasp, of course.

I think you are starting to understand too, however, that the gnarled old willow tree lived with a life-long ache. In fact, its ache was lives long if we're thinking in human terms. For from a sapling, it may have happily let a deer feast on its spring leaves then seen it suddenly start and dart and bounce along its escape route. And it couldn't help but imagine what that would be like – to be in different circumstances and vistas in an instant, or not to greet the sun at exactly the same angle every single day, and perhaps finally to see where the moon disappeared behind you.

What would that be like?

To be able to act and react on impulse: on a whim, on a hunch, on an instinct? The gnarled old willow tree's dream to be able to move freely was so far a fantasy that it only added to the ache.

What I've failed to tell you is that this special gnarled old willow tree lived not in a forest, nor in a wood, but in a garden. And that for many generations all the owners of the house in whose garden it grew had taken total delight in leaving this special willow tree to wend its way just as it had liked. So the twisting and gnarling was all of its own choice, however excruciatingly long each twist and turn might have taken it to make.

But then, one day, a new owner moved in: a small, frightened man with what might commonly be called 'control issues'. He found that the spooky sense the gnarled old willow tree evoked in him was something that he wanted rid of.

Short of chopping it straight down to its roots (he was small) he tried a host of devious horticultural tactics to get it at least a little bit in line – from pruning to poison, and even to pyrotechnics.

Yes, he scourged and purged and bound, as of course, it might be surmised, had been done to him at some point, somewhere in his sad little life.

Yet everything he did, the gnarled old willow tree withstood.

If it winced, it was only ever at bark level, never at core, never at root. It not only refused to be controlled but even rebelled and sometimes burst a whole new growth of root or branch like a tumour, to torment its owner – revenge returned in shooting spades.

'Keep pace, buddy…' it said as it saw the small and frightened man with his petrol can heading down the path again.

'I have the earth's power at my disposal. But you are even punier than you are,' as the old willow held its ground against another attempt to set to fire to it and turn it to dirt.

The little man persisted, determined, acting out his control game drama with perverted glee. This was a very sad thing indeed for anyone to have to see.

Let alone such a magnificent specimen of a wise, ancient tree to have to bear as a static wooden punching bag.

But the saddest thing of all about this time was that the gnarled old willow tree had no one to run up its core and hug its trunk and exchange the energy that gave it life. Yet it grew, I have to say (for it is undeniably true), far, far more in this sad time than when it kindly ached to cradle.

Anger and rebellion, it seems, can be the most excellent manure.

Then out of the blue one day, when the tree had almost forgotten the children and the kindness and the laughing sheer joy instead of venomous curses, it heard a voice that it had never heard before:

'You are lucky, Old Tree.'

The tree could have sworn the speaker was the house that shared the garden.

'I am?' the gnarled old willow asked, wondering how many years the house had sat there, silent, but watching everything from its windows.

'I have watched and seen,' the house confessed, 'but you are older than I and will outlive me, no doubt. Because this small man is pulling me apart from the inside out, wall by wall, beam by beam, and soon I will be just a crumbling shell…' The house's voice receded to a whisper.

And the gnarled old willow tree then realised that however long a life change took, even a very ancient tree could always change its life and live over, and over, and over again. Because it was eternal at root, fuelled by Mother Earth, and could never be turned to just dust and whispers and dirt, as bricks and mortar always would.

Years later, perhaps even centuries, a slice of that tree

told me this story in a riverside restaurant as it served me exquisite cheeses with the most delicious relishes.

We had a wonderful exchange.

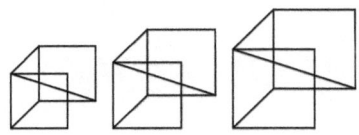

# The Battered but Beautiful Sailing Boat

Once upon a time there was a battered but beautiful sailing boat. Battered it was from years of ferrying clumsy day-trippers to any one of a handful of once-secret idyllic bays carved out by a mysterious Mediterranean coastline. Off they'd jump, some bold and bikinied, others stooped and aged and with a jump that was more of a stumble, but all of these steps would result in a violent jerk, chipping another few flakes off what was once a perfect Aegean blue hull.

But even now, years later, the sailing boat was still beautiful enough for its owner, young Giorgos. He would almost burst with pride whenever his feet turned on the winding path to the harbour.

There she was, and she was his.

Years ago, Giorgos had been orphaned by fortune when not much more than a babe and raised by the woods and the wind since (after he'd escaped the nuns, of course). So the battered but beautiful sailing boat had cradled his freedom gently in its aging hull like nothing else in this world ever had, or ever could. Little did he own now after buying her to offer as a means to restore her, but love he had in buckets to relish on her in the times that they shared.

For that, indeed, was his 'live for the day, come what may' attitude – the sort of attitude that keeps a person free and light-footed, for life.

Or for lifetimes.

The battered but beautiful sailing boat gave back all she could to her light-footed owner. She would arch her hull into the richest shoals of fish for him to catch with the ease of an expert conjurer, juggling slippery silver batons into her stern. She would hold him back from harnessing a good zephyr to charge him hard homeward when he'd had enough (but cause him to miss out on the sight of a dolphin pod at evening play). And she'd rock him to a magical slumber suited to the height of the midday sun's rays, swaying him to Old Mother Sea's rhythm as best as she could. And he would dream of times before the nuns. A skinny smiling Adonis: then, as now.

These were indeed idyllic times. In fact, if I hadn't spoken to them both independently, I might have thought it all a fantastic imagining, and harmless enough. But if it was an imagining, then they both had gotten their strange story very strangely straight...

You see, I was asked to interview them about the incident that happened one day, not so long ago, maybe a decade, maybe a lifetime or two, when they had sailed out to sea further than they'd ever been before. They both told me that it was a 'glory trip' as each felt the other would be lost to them soon – one to marriage, maybe, as it was certainly expected, and the other to the scrap yard, as similarly so. Endings of profound relationships take all sorts of strange and symbolic turns, and certainly this relationship took a very strange turn indeed.

Anyway, enough to say for now that the set of sail that day was bittersweet and their joint intent was more passionate and daring than it ever had been before. Well, perhaps not more than the few nights when Giorgos had taken a pretty girl out to the Blue Caves by torchlight, but we won't mention those. They were very few, and our battered but beautiful sailing boat turned a blind bow to them.

So, bear with me while I tell it, for a fantastic tale it is! I will give you the essence, as much more is incredible: the common themes of the stories they told me seemed to be that when they were far, far out to sea, much further than they had ever been, Poseidon himself rose up from the eternal inky waters, with his flashing trident in hand and a head full of sea snakes, just as the best story books depict. And with his great heavenly hand he steadied the prow of the battered but beautiful sailing boat into absolute pin-drop silent stillness. It was as if stillness itself stood still.

Both owner and boat were mesmerised, transfixed and totally suspended.

As you would be.

In fact, Giorgos, having spent enough time with the nuns to know his manners, would have bowed and said something suitably grand-sounding if he could. But his brain was just about alert enough to warn him of the possibility of a loss of control behind him, and his mouth seemed to have been stitched shut, so he stayed rudely upright as he was. Stock still, frozen, speechless, like a stone statue in front of an actual living God. But surely Gods don't need opening questions, he told himself in consolation.

Or perhaps not.

Because this frozen moment seemed to last as long as eternity – which of course would be silly, but so it felt. Maybe even more; it was certainly so long that it hurt like when you've had to hold your breath too long and you need to gasp or die.

Perhaps, Giorgos thought, he had.

And just then, as old folklore in many countries claims that the life you've lived will be shown to you just before you die, both Giorgos and his boat were treated to a cascade of their own life images. But not, in this instance, of how their lives had been, but of how from this day on they would, or perhaps could, be...

Giorgos saw his thickened limbs with grasping, wailing children hanging off them, and a wife who had rapidly aged to a bitter and wizened woman who never ever smiled – because he himself had broken her. And the battered but beautiful sailing boat saw its fate as a pile of rotting kindling, with a few lucky parts having managed to make up the bars of a sad rickety cage to keep sad rickety chickens in. And then it spotted an old odd piece of itself with a good strong nail sticking out of it, propped by the older Giorgos' door. For who knows what, but they both saw how it made a nice smack on his hand when he paced by the fire with it at night, drunk and angry. And the grasping, wailing children scattered, and his blank-faced wife wept, bitterly.

'You can stop these waves from reaching the shore,' Poseidon roared at the suspended pair, starting a small tsunami as he did so, as if for effect, and then calming it with his hot, moist breath: a father's gentle kiss to his wayward child.

'Stay free – if freedom truly is your journey,' and with those words he let their frozen spell be instantly freed too. At the very moment it was released, he slipped his monumental form beneath the surface of the inky waters, making no detectable ripple or wake, as if he had never been.

Gods tend to be like that – quizzical imposters, all of them. So, what was the reason for my interview with our heroes? Well, I was not the first and I doubt I will be the last to be fascinated by their story. But I was one of the lucky few to have found myself sitting on the harbour side and talking to them so candidly. It seemed I had waited there an eternity–maybe it was more.

You see, in the years since, and who knows how many there have been, young Giorgos and his battered but beautiful sailing boat have taken to living almost all their lives far out on the sea; not too far out, but far enough, only very rarely docking to replenish the small supplies they needed.

And small they were. For Giorgos returned to shore on that ominous and legendary day much changed and yet also not changed at all. For although countless days passed, he never did change in any way that even he could see, let alone others who whispered behind their hands as birthdays came and went, and came and went again, and the skinny Adonis stayed the same – apart from his smile.

As eventually, of course, so did all his friends and family, and all the girls he'd taken out to the Blue Caves by torchlight: they came and they went.

So perhaps I could report that if your future flashes before you, do please be aware that all you may be able to do is live forever in the moment after that. Although I am quite sure it all depends on the future that you see, of course.

Staying free from your future's curse, you may well be cursed to be free. Curses and wishes are equally as quizzical as Gods, you see.

And what became of our battered but beautiful sailing boat, you might ask – was she magically restored by Poseidon's grasp to her former glory? Was she perfect Aegean blue with sails as pristine laundered sheets, for all eternity?

Of course not – that would be ridiculous.

But as I watched Giorgos pack his few supplies for the next few months (or maybe lifetimes) I couldn't help letting my fingers try to pick a flake from the battered but beautiful sailing boat's hull when I was sure that he, and she, weren't looking.

'You'll need the strength of a God,' I thought I heard the boat whisper.

Or maybe it came from the sea.

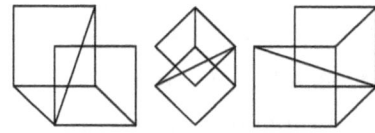

# For the FLIGHT

*Tales to relax into, for the fantasy of 'happily ever after'…*

# The Magical Candle

Once upon a time there was a magical candle that lived in the lounge of a bachelor pad. Now this wasn't the first place the candle had lived. It had been through quite a journey to get to Tony's coffee table to sit, at a slightly wonky over-burnt angle, next to an African fertility sculpture and a mosaic box from Morocco where Tony hid his special cigarettes.

This pretty aromatic candle had enjoyed many views in its lifetime, but Tony's bachelor pad was perhaps the most entertaining of them all.

Because the magical candle would be lit on those special evenings when Tony 'entertained' a young lady; not that Tony was young himself, but two divorces, three kids and a short membership of Alcoholics Anonymous later found him looking for a soul mate in the pages of the classifieds, or on his computer, or even on late night TV satellite channels.

The magical candle saw his searching and she wanted to help.

Yes, she saw it all. She saw the pizza delivery guy a lot; and how often Tony slept on the sofa, and the back of a collection of empty whisky bottles he seemed to like to make. She knew a special evening was on the cards when they'd disappear all of a sudden. She assumed they were precious and he put them away somewhere for safe keeping.

Sadly, the magical candle would never be lit apart from on these nights; probably because there wasn't much left of her to light. The first inch of her wick and wax had been burnt in brief bouts beside a Buddha and a treasured photo of an old Indian man sitting in what looked a very painful way, by an intense girl who liked to finger beads and gaze without blinking on her flame. But quite often the girl would start to cry at those times and quickly snuff her out. Once our magical candle was even drowned out by floods of hot tears that soaked right down her wick and made her feel more on fire than she'd ever been.

Suddenly the girl had packed a ridiculously sized rucksack and bought a ticket to India. And along with the girl's kitchen knick-knacks and hand knitted mohair jumpers, the magical candle ended up in a charity shop with a sticker on it for 50p.

That was when Tony's sister had seen it. She was trying to relight the spark in her tired marriage, not least to be a good example to her brother, but also to be a good girl for her parents who couldn't face another child of theirs getting divorced. Not in this lifetime. Now, this pretty aromatic candle was just the perfect thing to put on the table with the beef bourguignon and bottle of Barolo she hoped would also work their charm that night. At that stage our magical candle had at least four inches left to burn, and a lot can be done with that if the setting is right.

So that night the magical candle glowed with all its might. And the long-married couple saw each other as the lovers who had met in their teenage years again. She flickered in a way that wiped out their wrinkles better than the best Botox. She even managed to warm them in a way that reminded them of the Sardinian sun on the holiday they'd taken when they had got married on a whim in a little white chapel with only two cleaners and two candles as witnesses.

'How special,' thought the magical candle as she was carefully pinched by the moist, slightly trembling fingertips of the man who would soon be using a similar move to spark other things into life.

And so it was something of a shock the very next day to be given to Tony, who at that time smelt less than aromatic, and made a face at her like *she* was the bad smell. He unceremoniously dumped her on top of a pile of empty pizza boxes in the hall. There she stayed for quite a while, joined at some point by a bottle of aftershave and a designer shirt, both from Tony's sister, who never took her back because she was far too busy beaming and glowing and showing off air tickets to Sardinia. The magical candle had been here before: shelved or – at best – up for the recycling pile.

But then one day, just as the candle had decided that it might be quite nice to see the salad servers and corkscrew shaped like a piglet that it had left on the shelf in the charity shop, Tony went into a frantic frenzy. And she was moved first onto the window ledge, then onto the top of the TV, and then finally she came to rest on the coffee table next to the African statue, that actually seemed quite friendly despite a tongue that looked like a serpent on acid.

After a few short hours, she heard the familiar laughter of a young female (as occasionally her first owner had smoked a joint) and a few clangs of wineglasses on the table that reverberated under her pleasantly. And then she was lit, and she worked her charm, and the voices softened and whispered and became moans and kisses, and she was snuffed out with moist, slightly trembling fingers and knew that her job was, again, done.

This happy ritual went on for weeks: different giggles every time, but the same result. It was odd that she never saw the girl in the morning (or the same girl twice for that matter) but she was doing her job and she was doing it just fine.

Then one evening, in the middle of the wine glass reverberations, she was unexpectedly whisked away from the African statue. She was mid-air, floating, so close to Tony's stubble she could tell he'd finally used that aftershave.

'Let me see you.' She heard an older woman's smoky voice and saw a hand that was wrinkled and actually rather misshapen gently stroke Tony's bristles and outline his lips before he uncurled its fingers and kissed its palm tenderly.

'We don't have to…' she heard the older woman whisper to him gently, '…in fact, I'd rather we didn't. I'd rather we just talked.'

'Yes…me too…' Tony said with a sigh the magical candle had never heard before. Not from Tony anyway.

Then just as the last millimetre of her melted away, she couldn't help but fret and panic madly that she hadn't worked her charm in her finale, that in her last chance to shine, she'd failed; she'd lost all her power so it was just as well she was dying away, anyway.

Poor Tony – destined to be alone, forever.

But in her last few seconds of life, a vague memory of the day that she was made flickered briefly across her wick as she spluttered out – of an older woman who lived by the sea and who, with every candle that she lovingly crafted with her arthritic hands, cast a true wish into the moulding setting wax that one, just one magical candle, might one day light her way home.

# The Creaking, Tired Old Bed Frame

Once upon a time there was a creaking, tired old bed frame – the kind that everyone dreads when they've longed for a silent night's sleep, and would happily trade their right arm for a bit of peace and quiet by 2am.

This creaking, tired old bed frame had seen very many years of service and over the years had developed something of a sigh that was all of its own. It was a rather mournful wail with a sloping, stepping down tone whenever anyone sat on it, which made you think that it might have lost its life partner years before but never gotten over it, or perhaps just broken the very last plate from its favourite dinner service.

What a shame. Poor, exhausted bed frame.

You'd think it was long past its time to become firewood, or rest its ornate bed head in the likes of an old barn store until the worms got to it, wouldn't you?

But, it just so happened that this creaking, tired old bed frame was lucky – or unlucky – enough, to have been solidly built into the walls of a top class business hotel. And so, because it was part of the original features, the mountain of paperwork required to renovate it really wasn't worth it, according to the manager who thought paperwork was for bonfires at best. As some sort of five star remedy, his idea was to build big, brash, sound bouncing speakers into the bedsides, so that corporate types could dock their iPods, and so drown out the mournful wail of the bed frame; at least until they were deeply asleep and making a fair few mournful wails of their own, anyway.

So, most occupants of the room never even noticed it. They'd be You Tubing on the 52 inch plasma screen, or shuffling a playlist to keep them awake whilst they rewrote their presentations because their petty-minded bosses had infuriatingly dictated that they had to, at the last minute, without quite telling them why. Or maybe they'd be Skyping someone erotically, who they thought was exotic and, whose squeaks were the only ones they were tuned into.

Whatever the distraction, the true sound of their surroundings was pretty easily drowned out by the souped-up soundtrack that, sadly, seemed to be the automatic accompaniment to all their noisy, demanding lives. It just seemed to be the way with the corporate types who stayed in the creaking, tired old bed frame's room – loud and distracted souls, not at all observant of the tired old bed frame's creaks.

The manager clearly knew his clientele well.

Then one day, a lady stayed in the room. She had worked hard and long in the tough corporate world for years – too many to remember, but with too few left to feel that she could do anything else. But the stress of the keeping up was really catching up with her. Utterly exhausted as she stumbled through the door with her trusty wheeled suitcase which she let collapse onto its face on the floor (just as she wanted to), within minutes she was peeling off the severe control underwear she hooked herself into daily and sliding into the soft fluffy bathrobe, loosely tied, instead.

But before she let herself sink onto the bed she was longing for, carefully she removed and matched up her earrings and backs, and then she even more carefully unpicked the tiny hearing aids that she wove through her hairline each morning, so that no one would see why she sometimes took a little bit longer to participate in discussions than her eager, younger 'pick me, I'm brilliant!' colleagues who had no understanding of silence.

And then she let herself flop down heavily, not at all prettily, into the creaking, tired old bed frame, keeling like an elephant shot with a dart. And as she landed, heavy-backed and legs flailing, she felt in her heart the echo of a strange, mournful wail of understanding as the tired old bed frame embraced her, richly and deeply.

'Oh, you beautiful bed!' she sighed, with a sloping, stepping down tone. And she swam deliciously in its cool sheets and did a few backstrokes, and leg swishes, which prompted a whole new range of creaks and groans, which of course she didn't hear.

Not even a squeak.

But she *felt* the bed sing with her, and somehow, her vibration must have been exactly in harmony with the bed frame itself for although she couldn't hear it, I swear that as she told the story to me, I heard the very lowest note of a cello, slow and deep and soothing. Like a bow that had finally touched its long lost string.

And a perfect night's sleep followed, one you'd trade both arms, and a leg, for.

Or maybe the most profound trade that was made on that night was an instant love for something misfit and misplaced, swapped for the spark of a perfect idea. Yes, at something like two in the morning our quiet tired lady made a silent promise to herself to exchange her creaking tired old corporate life for a small, quiet, bijou gift store in the countryside. A silent promise she would take very seriously immediately after her Blackberry rudely vibrated her awake the next morning.

And for many years after our lady would enjoy the hunt to find a bed that was just like our beautiful, tired old bed frame. These were much, much happier days for her – not just because of the fun of the hunt, but because she never once had to hook herself into severe control underwear, or weave secret aids up into her hairline to hear corporate discussions that frankly bored her rigid anyway.

And, though many wondered why she would bother, she took lessons to learn to play the cello.

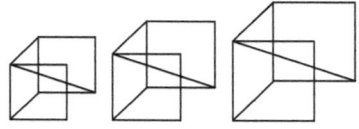

# The Little Mound of Flesh

Once upon a time there was a little mound of flesh. In truth it was the most insignificant bit of anatomy compared to say, the grandeur of the glorious heart muscle, or the complexity of the skeletal structure, or the computer-like blancmange of the brain. But this tiny little mound certainly had a mind all of its own. At least, it did have a mind of its own, if the owner of the body it protruded from at some ecstatic moment had a mind to find it...

For there were a myriad of valid reasons why the little mound might stay hidden or completely un-awakened – yes, even for a lifetime. Truly, yes. For frankly, it didn't enjoy the luxury of an immediately accessible location like the index finger of the left hand; although often they laughed about that when their paths finally crossed. And it wasn't like a nose, all stuck out there and obvious, although some noses would have given a nostril to swap places, given the very nasty ridicule they could attract. Anyway, the little mound of flesh was tucked away, hidden and sheltered and far out of harm's way, wherever 'harm' might be, from a rather hard bicycle seat, to a roving teenage boy's over-eager teeth. Hidden as it was, it still had a lot to handle at times!

Occasionally, the little mound would pop out to play and would raise a loud and sudden orchestra of feelings as it was soaped in the shower or it had a heated tussle with a tough seam on a pair of jeans, or was accidentally on purpose (who could say?) leaned against the washing machine on a high spin cycle. Then truly it had a voice all of its own, that would cause the whole body that owned it to groan from deep down low, and purr like a cat that hadn't just got the cream but a mouthful of caviar washed down with champagne and a tug on a great joint, and maybe the keys to a magical kingdom too.

The point of this story is that the little mound of flesh didn't often come out to play. It could even be a once-in-a-lifetime thing. Truly, yes. Because despite it proudly knowing all the other names for the important major limbs and joints and muscles, it still wasn't quite sure of its own little name. It thought it might be something like 'Delores', but that sounded wrong and more like a mad gypsy you might meet at the fun fair with jangling bracelets and rolling rrrs and ridiculous promises of the future, or so the left ear lobe had told her once. She liked the left ear lobe – it sometimes got nibbled too, and didn't always like how that felt, either. Now, the right ear lobe...well, that's another story...

Anyway, to not know your own name can be a very frightening thing. For who's to know if when you're out to play at the playground's edge and someone calls a warning, whether it's for you or not? You might carry on playing and stick your neck out too far and get your head bitten off.

Now that wouldn't do anyone any good, would it?

And it's even more frightening that whenever you think that someone might actually be talking about you, it's in hushed tones or in a very silly name that you know isn't yours at all, so it's also remarkably confusing for just a small mound of flesh to cope with. In fact, right ear lobe had said that hushed tones and silly names are generally only used when something is very sick, so sick that everyone knows it's going to die soon, and something about a 'c-word', so the little mound of flesh began to think that its days of popping out to play were probably numbered on the fingers of the left hand – and however good a friend the left hand was, this train of thought wasn't very reassuring.

And so it took a decision: which really isn't easy when you're not well-equipped for decision-making, and most of your nature is just hard-wired for pleasure. But one day, it decided, whilst its owner was on a long haul flight, that it would ask for help to play away its last days in total pleasure and low gasps and orchestras of delight. It might as well go with a bang, as they say.

Sadly, at the moment of this decision, which was fleeting as there wasn't much resource to fuel it, most of the rest of its owner's body was deep and fast asleep. Even the usually friendly left hand fingertips which were resting in tantalisingly close proximity, wedged between its owner's thighs and the seatbelt buckle, could not be tempted awake to play. And the glorious, grand heart muscle had slowed its pace right down to the point of the occasional blip, but nothing more...and the complex computer-like blancmange of the brain had its sign hung up: 'Out to lunch; back on landing impact,' displayed in dull neon behind its owner's eyelids.

So who would play?? In these moments that the little mound of flesh felt might even be its very last – largely because making its decision had drained it of all its energy like a chef squeezing out spinach – who would help to make the wonderful rich purr of the cat that got the cream and maybe the kingdom?

'Hello' said the dreamscape.

'Oh, who are you?' asked the little mound of flesh.

'I'm everywhere you want to go, and every way you want to play, and everyone you want to meet...ever.'

'Are you? Are you really?'

'Truly,' said the dreamscape, drifting around and under and over its owner, like beautifully fragrant smoke, weaving images and scenes randomly, prompted by a shuffling iPod plugged in just above left and right ear lobes – who were frankly not best pleased to be forced to stay awake for the whole transatlantic trip, but at least it drowned out the duty free messages a bit.

And the little mound of flesh found itself feeling suddenly totally and absolutely alive, as if it hadn't just discovered a new playmate, but a whole new country. In fact, it felt like a complete switch of planet, from one where you breathe air and walk on earth, to one where you can breathe under water and fly. Or at least, a world where all walkways are on a moving belt which, coincidentally, its owner had just enjoyed at the airport, especially as it had wobbled at just the right vibration and lurched her forward at the sudden shocking 'Mind your step!' which had made both the little mound and its owner gasp a laugh and beam a lasting smile.

'How beautiful is this window opening from an Italian villa onto that sunset?' asked the dreamscape.

'Wondrous' was the little mound's response, feeling reached-for from behind.

'Is this knight who knows exactly where to find you even before his armour's been fully peeled from his body a delight to you?'

'Joy beyond compare,' came the cry.

'And is your name even needed when the soft mouth upon you whispers "Perfect...delicious...come with me"?'

And the little mound of flesh was speechless, purring.

All it could do was feel utterly eternal, a part of another dimension, completely.

Because it now knew that however small, however hidden it was, it lived a life, however long, however fleeting, that even heart and brain and both hands – and certainly left and right ear lobes – could only ever hope to dream of.

Hours later, when its owner finally awoke, it was with quite a different spring in her transatlantic step and a new liking for longhaul flights.

She also planned a trip to Italy just as soon as she could.

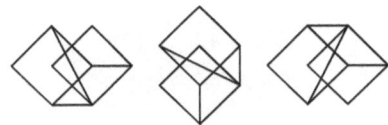

# The Feel Good Refrain

Once upon a time there was a feel good refrain: a happy, skippy tune that everybody past a certain age would know and would sometimes find themselves whistling whilst they were changing the oil on the car, or some such. The feel good refrain had a simple way of charming cheer into the whistler or singer within just a few bars, and a lightness of step would follow that, if it hadn't been likely to raise the risk of tripping over in front of the neighbours, might even have developed into a full-on skip.

Well, maybe...

But the feel good refrain had a big chip on its shoulder. It had once been stolen by a seventies rock band as the basis for a sweeping anthem of a number one hit. But by the time that every layer had been dubbed and over-dubbed, the simple notes of the light-hearted, feel good refrain had been drowned to death in a crescendo of wailing backing singers, bass effects and a legendary drum break which had been thumped out on just about every car steering wheel in the land. It had simply got lost in the drama of it all, and now it felt totally redundant.

It had never wanted to be dramatic. And it had never wanted to be associated with men in Lycra suits and makeup, locked in a crazy decade that it felt should be forgotten – a view which most of those who remembered it tended to agree with. All this meant that the feel good refrain was trapped: stuck in a time warp that was not of its making. It felt like a bit of a grubby secret, brought out just for a laugh on karaoke stag nights. And most of all, it had never wanted to be the subject of ridicule.

So through no fault of its own it had ended up having a life that it didn't want. Yes, it was now grand and flashy and glitzy, but it didn't want to be. And so every time it hummed to itself the dozen or so notes that made up its core, it would find itself welling up in the way grandpas who realise that they've missed the best time in their own kids' lives do. And it would choke, and not even be able to finish its own song. It felt tragic and wasted and past its sell-by-date, and so much less than it had really wanted to be.

All its life it had imagined that it might become a simple, soft nursery rhyme that was sung through the generations, from grandmother to grandchild, gently lulling and shushing and sending fragile new lives back to the most magical of sleeps. It had the idea that it had something eternal to offer, something to hand on like a treasured heirloom that no one even knew the source of. Small and precious as a trinket, meaningless to anyone but those who owned it, never defined by one era or society, and flexible enough to find its way into the mental music box of anyone, anywhere.

But instead it was stuck in a Lycra bodysuit and drowned out in reverb effect.

One day it found itself being hummed by a doll-like Chinese classical violin student, in its absolutely purest form, the very way it longed for, the way it had almost given up hope of, as she pottered about her attic loft.

This loft was cluttered to the rafters with piles of musical scores and compilations. And a million grubby coffee cups and a matching set of teacups.

And as she hummed, and the feel good refrain basked in joy, the doll-like violinist was shuffling a pile of pieces like old family photos or a box of precious keepsakes, carefully laying each one aside to form another pile in the just sufficient space she'd shunted between two others.

'I think it's you!' and she nursed a piece of sheet music with delight and leapt over several piles with the expertise of someone who was accustomed to living in artistic chaos.

She popped the score onto her music stand, which was shaped like two swans kissing and which she'd had since her very first violin lesson, when she'd been so small she'd had to stand up on a pile of manuscripts to use it. Piles can have their uses at times, you see.

And then she played. And she played note-perfectly. Yes, she played the very notes she was humming with such an exquisite clarity and lightness that it sent the feel good refrain off surfing waves of silent, awe-struck paroxysms.

It could do nothing else but watch, as each note glowed on the page with an intense luminosity: like watching a firework trail in a slow motion movie, or every single degree of a shooting star's course.

'Mozart! I knew it!' she exclaimed, and gave a little skip of delight as she went off to make a huge amount of coffee in a receptacle that was vaguely sanitary. She was going to need it, as she'd just been commissioned to compose a piece for a new children's opera with an impossible deadline. Now she had the beautiful hook she needed to fuel her creation; she just needed a bucket load of caffeine to finish it.

All the while she clattered around in her kitchenette she was still humming, and the still quivering melody stared and gawped at the pattern of black dots and curly swirls dangling from five straight lines on the yellowing page. They were all still illuminating, still throbbing in perfect rhythm with her humming and la-la-la-ing; it was its own true energy that the feel good refrain had almost forgotten it had heard or seen or felt before.

And then it heard and saw and felt something even stranger to its reality.

A decrepit old man who looked like a tramp appeared like a vapour in the corner of the attic. The Chinese girl shivered and closed the skylight and hugged her coffee mug.

But she didn't see the weather-beaten tramp man, who looked to the feel good refrain perhaps very ill, maybe even dying, but who smiled the unmistakable smile of a proud father, or maybe grandfather, or maybe something more.

'I found you in a child's song in a meadow...' he whispered, croakily, 'and the part you have to play may have only just begun...' as he disappeared, wistfully.

In the half light of the glowing trail of itself the feel good refrain suddenly deserved its own name, as it knew that one lifetime locked in a Lycra-clad time-warp cannot have any effect on a melody that has no beginning or end.

# The Little Patch of Earth

Once upon a time there was a little patch of earth, so small that most people who walked past this patch never even saw it. Or if they did, it was often in a 'corner of the eye' kind of way, or without focus, like when you've watched too many adverts or political debates. It had longed to be part of a mountain, or at least a hill in its day – but had learnt to settle for its lot as time had gone by.

Because, you see, this little patch of earth happened to be positioned between a bustling pavement and a cold, hard concrete wall, in the shade, on a sharp corner, where the world just whistled past it. And the patch had nothing blossoming in it that could possibly catch a whistling person's eye.

But what no one bustling by on the pavement knew was that this little patch of barren looking earth happened to have buried deep within its very nature the potential to grow the most beautiful shade-defying blooms. Not just strong blooms, or tall blooms, but blooms with such a beauty that the bustling, whistling passers-by would be forced to stop and each would oddly take a deep breath, and then go more gently on their way, often quite reluctantly, looking over their shoulders to catch a glimpse of such a rare beauty once more, just in case it had faded by the time they walked by again, or to check that they hadn't imagined it.

At least, this was the dream of the little patch of earth.

And the passers-by needn't fear that it would be a one-off when it happened. For the power in the little patch of earth was gleaned from years of being the sort of place where maybe a little mouse might choose to go to lie down its last time, or where a spider might decide to weave its most wonderful web ever, or where a baby bird far from its nest could safely rest and somehow be invisible to all roaming predators, until its mother scooped it safely back under her wing. This patch was a very special place to those creatures who were able to see it.

But so far, this was all ultimately untested. Our little patch lay sadly barren, to those with this world eyes.

The little patch longed daily to give all its potential to a glorious bloom – a flower that it could enjoy growing with, as much as the passers-by would admire it. It had tried, but sometimes when a seed had started to germinate, it had shot up far too quickly and toppled itself over, or some seeds had been sadly overwhelmed by the throb in the earth around it, and too frightened of this strange place even to start to bloom. Because this earth was not the usual earth and seeds meant to be earthbound did know that they were. And on one very sad occasion, the little patch, in sheer frustration and longing, had pushed a blousy, showy bloom way beyond its real potential, and then finally found that it proved to be a weed, and that it propagated itself so busily and deeply that it sucked the patch's special nourishment in a way it really shouldn't have.

So, the patch had learnt to be very careful about what it tried to grow now.

And in those times when the patch had to lie fallow again

to restore itself in the shade, it would look at the blooms not very far away from its edges and wonder, 'Why can't that beauty be mine?' Then it would weep, and in so doing wash away old dead roots. It would sigh and so blow away dead, dry seed heads. In this way it would clear its ground. So then a frog might hop onto the patch and whisper its throaty, croaky thanks for the wonderful cool and life-giving shade the little patch offered, and the strange magic of this very special spot of earth would start to renew itself, again.

Then, out of the blue, one day when the little patch had been looking longingly at the blooms along the way all day, a passer-by who often whistled this way, stopped still. His feet usually very nearly ran past the patch at a pelt with the kind of walk that wiggles with a panic, pulled by work and guilt and fear, and creates a patter all of its own. But today he stopped. He actually knelt. He touched the path to bury something in it. It was a ring – a diamond solitaire which was still warm from his pocket. Yet this stunning sparkling ring had dark sadness stuck all over it.

"I won't need this," he said, "...there!" and he thumped amd stamped the earth.

Then his patter turned suddenly angry, sad, hurt and ashamed all in one. He turned and ran very quickly away with a force that nearly tore the earth asunder under wherever his feet hit it.

Instantly, the little patch felt very scared. It felt too full of something that surely had no right to be hidden, too at risk of a magpie pecking into its heart to scavenge it, or maybe of a wronged ex-passer by turning up, who would burrow into it and kick it all over the pavement in rage, where it would never have a hope of getting itself back together again. And if that horrible scattered fate happened, it would also never be deep enough to hold a beautiful bloom – it would just be spread around and ground down on the soles of the shoes of passers-by forever. It was terrified, and so it determined to make what it felt must be a wrong, right.

So, for the next few days, full up and scared and panicked, the only thing the little patch could think of was to make sure that whenever the panicked passer by passed by, it drew his attention in some way and reminded him of his treasure. All it felt that it had at its disposal was bits of grit and gravel, and maybe the odd tiny, empty snail shell to somehow spit up into his path.

But oddly, and suddenly, it felt that the most beautiful flower then bloomed, without a second's effort. A flower that had its own strength and a perfect height, and a way of defying the shade that gave it truly a diamond sparkle in that dark little corner between the concrete wall and the pavement. The little patch beamed with pride because it could finally do what it had so longed to do after all. Bloom and blossom, grow and give life.

Daily it would hear the passers-by and their panic patter, with the very slightest pause once in an occasional while, that would get very slightly longer each time the pause broke the patter. Until one day, maybe a week or maybe a year later (because little patches of earth are not very good at all at keeping time or scores) that same passer-by stopped, and the passer-by actually knelt, and the passer-by reached in to find his ring and said:

'I'd almost forgotten that you were here. I'd certainly lost hope that I'd ever need you!'

As he scooped the earth back in its place and patted it

kindly, the little patch asked him as best as earth can, and rather breathy with over-excitement:

'Did you see it? Did you see my bloom?'

As if he had heard the earth (although he hadn't, as bustling passers-by are not very good at all at listening to the earth) the smiling passer-by stood up on his now-steady and still legs with strongly grounded feet and said:

'Thank you for being totally inconspicuous. You are the most beautiful patch of earth that I have ever seen. You never needed a bloom to be special to me – and forever you will be'

The little patch realised that the longed for admiration of the passers-by for what it could grow or how it compared to other patches of earth, meant nothing but dry dust and weeds.

And that what it now realised it had imagined it had grown could have been picked within an instant, spoilt within a second, and trash within a week anyway.

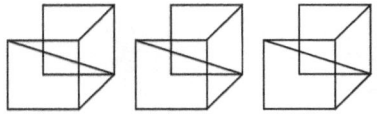

# The Matching Antique Chairs

Once upon a time there was a pair of matching antique chairs. And they'd been a splendidly grand pairing in their day, framing the entrance hall of a five star chateau in France, no less. With their pristine upholstery and gleaming, gilded feet, they proudly stood, sentry-like, on either side of the most regal and awe-inspiring gravity-defying floral displays. And many a guest would rest their tourist-tired limbs from yet another vineyard visit, draping themselves with an elegance they relished whilst their loved one finally finished in the bathroom.

But those days had long gone. Because over many years, through a series of bankruptcies and country house sales and market square auctions and several trips wrapped in old blankets in the back of a workman's van, they now found themselves on display in the window of a converted barn store in a small village in England, with a shabby chic label and a vulgar price tag to match.

'Who on earth would pay such a price for us in this condition?' they wondered.

It was shameful. Like being presented to the Pope in your old pyjamas, or going on a first date with the very worst cold sores eating up your top lip.

But purchased at full price they were – by a bonnie young girl who fell in love with them as she drove past one day. They were perfect in her eyes, as she was looking for something to make her clients feel different and distracted and very special indeed as they waited at her clinic.

Because her clients were all very sick, you see: so sick that all they'd had to look at in the last few months, perhaps even years, were clinical walls and drips, and all they'd been able to think about about was whether all the medical paraphernalia would work in their cases. Lifesavers magic bullets and gizmos certainly can be, but in the case of all the bonnie young girl's clients, sadly they hadn't been.

But it so happened that the bonnie young girl knew an awful lot about life-saving. You see, she was married to a life-saver: a marvellous hunk of a man she'd met at the local ball three years before, who by day farmed pigs and muck-shifted, but by night he revived discarded beams or long-dead tree stumps into new archways or doors, or arms and legs for flailing disabled furniture. He'd even made their marriage bed (he started the night he met her) by restoring a couple of old railway sleepers. Sometimes she said she could hear a hoot and a whistle when he went like a train. With hands that were calloused from hauling pig carcasses daily, over months he'd lovingly carved a delicate swooping dragonfly into the headboard, and often they would both hang onto its wings.

When the life-saver saw the pair of antique chairs his bonnie young girl had bought, he let out one of his hoots:

'You darling!' For he knew the love with which his girl had bought them, not just for him but for so many. And she'd removed the price tag and was very good at distraction tactics.

That night he took that love, their love, and his love for

the workmanship he could see, and magnified it as much as he could and stitched it deep down into the very core of the first of the chairs. He riveted in love right around the seat, locking in the softest deep pile velvet he could find. And he returned the feet from worn- thin claws to rounded-padding paws. And then one night he gilded the first antique chair from head to toe – a messy job that needed two, so he and his girl shared a bottle of golden bubbles in the draughty barn studio as they got a bit gilded themselves, stopping occasionally for the odd chink of glass and lips along the way. That was the deal. He was no idiot.

Now, it was nearly Christmas and the girl had done everything she could to cheer her clinic waiting lounge – lights and stars and angels twinkled with the hope of heavenly magic in the very darkest time. But somehow, still it didn't feel enough.

So she twisted the lifesaver's arm (which he rather enjoyed as it usually meant he could twist hers back) and he shunted both chairs across the barn to the waiting lounge: one pristine and gleaming, and one still shabby chic and cold-sore scabby and frankly profoundly embarrassed to be anywhere near its now very far from identical twin.

'What a beauty!' was the favourite exclamation of the day as patients parcelled in with mince pies and brandy snaps made with the love of a last batch. Tears welled up easily for many of them now, and the life-saving love they saw in the restored chair had them gazing and clasping hands to mouths and bitten lips, and silently wishing for the bonnie young girl and her husband a protection that would keep them gilded forever – even if such luck was not to be their own lot.

'Sit in me!' begged the gilded chair, '…please!' to all the clients who passed it.

It was silently aching to hold and support those so in

need of some comfort and rest, but who were now bizarrely standing for far too long in reverent respect for its splendour.

Sit they would, as if they'd heard its cry – but not in it. They would all, without exception, sag into the tired shabbiness of its twin.

One by one, in fact every one, every single one, would in turn, turn.

Yes, they treasured the beauty of the gilded restored chair from afar, no doubt of that, but they all relished the comfort of the version that felt far more 'right' to sit in, far more 'them'. And some would even give a little pat to the chair they had chosen to sit in, with a comforting stroke and a whisper:

'Your turn next…'

But somehow the bonnie young girl never did push for her lifesaver husband to work his magic on the second chair. Perhaps she'd noticed how no one sat in the gilded one and she couldn't afford to lose two seats on busy clinic days. Or perhaps she realised that in their odd combination they served the best purpose.

Or maybe, most likely, she was focused on the crib that the lifesaver was carving now as he'd worked an entirely different kind of life-saving magic in their lives. He was busy weaving baby dragonflies dancing a wish of sweet dreams about their soon to be first born crib's edges, so I'm sure we can forgive her for leaving the other chair behind.

Although, from the lonely tone of its story and the golden glow of a different kind I felt from its antique twin, I'm not convinced that the gilded antique chair did.

# For the FRIGHT

*Tales with a twist, for when you need a darker touch...*

# The Bully in a Pinstripe Suit

Once upon a time there was a big fat bully in a pinstripe suit. Now, that probably doesn't sound very kind. And it is a little unfair as he wasn't the size of an oil tanker or anything like that. But he was rather weirdly shaped, with a protruding paunch falling from his lady-sized shoulders, a bully's belly which had a habit of pushing its way right into your space, which meant that you actually had to reverse a bit to accommodate it.

So even before the bullying began, you were on the back foot, off-balance, on guard just from looking at him; which was a good thing really, because the bullying would start within seconds of you meeting him. He'd throw out vile attacking verbal tricks and twists, and then add bullish, blinkered judgements that you just couldn't argue with; not before another one bashed you about the head.

Conversations with him were like catching a hand grenade with no pin in it, with one hand covered in soap suds and the other forced up your back.

And somehow he had the knack of pulling just the right facial expression that made you feel like a speck of dust he might just blow away in disgust, with a wet sneeze to follow that he'd wipe on his sleeve. Some people said it had something to do with the way his eyes seemed to go in different directions. And even his pinstripes were forced to pull in different directions, trying to accommodate his peculiar paunchy shape. Which meant however well-turned-out he was, he had the permanent look of just coming from a bar room brawl or shaping up to start one; probably, with you.

Yes, if you'd had to pick him out of a line up of 'best in show' bullies, or a movie director had been casting a non-speaking character part, he'd have come top of the class for carrying that off with the ease of a 'born to play it' bit part.

Now this big fat bully ran a company. Well, 'ran' is a flattering word as that implies a degree of management and the ability to move fast. The big fat bully didn't see either as part of his job. In fact, no one really knew what he did see as his job, except for scaring the stomach contents and steady heart rhythms out of his senior management team, and then lying to the bank about returns on investment that would never come good; the latter being something that everybody knew (even the receptionist), but the bank somehow didn't.

His job seemed to be to paunch himself about in a cloud of threats and deceit and bizarreness and also to manage (we are using the term loosely here) to somehow only do this for maybe three days a week. Yet he also had the unnerving ability to pounce on anyone who downed tools or closed laptops before some unreasonable hour in the evening. And of course, there was never a question of overtime payment.

There was a joke that maybe one of his eyes was watching you all the time while the other one was lining up his golf ball on the eighteenth tee.

So, 'bizarre' is really the kindest word I can use to describe this bully. He was definitely not a candidate for the usual pinstriped boss' perks: no receptionist or marketing manager made it in their interest to seduce him in the hope of special favours. For they'd heard of his reputation, and feared a weirdness might continue between the sheets. Can you imagine? Well, everyone who did (and they all tried very hard not to) shuddered and frankly veered close to vomiting.

But as with all bullies, there is a come-uppance encounter to this tale. Because the bully in a pinstripe suit was so busy hunting for blame and fault and fraud that he didn't factor in the power of the gentle care that one of his team possessed.

This man was a farmer – not literally you understand, as most farmers don't don pinstripes at 5am and focus their lives on blackberries made of plastic. It was more that his *mindset* was of the faithful farmer, trusting that when good seeds were planted and nurtured, even in the very grimmest ground, a strong harvest just had to follow. It was a law of nature he'd trusted unquestioningly all his life. Yes, it is clear that the faithful farmer's mindset could not have been further removed from the bully's way of thinking than a stick of smooth pure white chalk is from the jagged blades of a cheese grater.

And as fate would have it, in the ironic way it likes, this farmer was as addicted to ploughing his particular furrow in life as the bully was to pummelling his.

So even the big fat bully was tended and nurtured by the faithful farmer – he just couldn't help it! Yes, a shoot of anything that resembled empathy or understanding was hedged about with special fencing and watered carefully and kept safe under a cloche until the faithful farmer felt it was time to look at it again and check its progress. Sometimes he'd take a peek and the shoot had withered to a mouldy stinking dust or been eaten by weird looking (quite paunchy) grubs. And he'd be disappointed, of course, and sometimes even quite depressed. But inevitably he'd find himself raking the ground over and sowing yet again, driven by his utter faith in the power of the harvest.

So, the come-uppance came one day when they were on some corporate jolly roaming through vineyards of a supplier in Spain whose best bottles the big fat bully was salivating at the chance of getting his sweaty palms on. If only he could just screw the terms and conditions of the supplier's agreement a sneaky bit further in his favour, but make it look exactly the opposite, of course.

And the farmer, who was tired of tilling the barren soil of the bully today and had just decided to relish the beauty of a real life harvest, happened to stop at a tiny little truck, too small to hold anything you could really call a harvest, except for a few bunches of grapes and a little blue wellington boot.

And he joked with the supplier, whose son was the proud truck driver:

'It all starts there, doesn't it?'

And the supplier said, laughing back, 'He'll be king of all this one day, and more. I'm so proud of him. So proud that he's my son.'

And he beamed.

And the power of the light of that smile that the farmer and supplier shared cut right through the big fat bully's belly like a steaming hot sword through butter that's been left out all day.

Shafting it went, swiftly up through his ribcage, with a searing hot tip reaching high into the left ventricle of his heart and then weaving its way down his left arm in a pain that he'd never felt before, at least not physically, and at least not for very many years.

As he crumpled to his knees begging for someone to please, please help him, he saw his legs in pinstripe pyjamas and his little feet in tiny blue wellington boots. And a pool of dark stinging hot water appeared at his feet.

'You screw-eyed fat freak of nature! You're not my son...still pissing in your pants at your age! You'll be a nothing, a nobody...If you ever make me proud I'd likely die in shock on the spot, you little shit...'

And in the agonising eternal moments that the crumpled up bully spent slumped over his paunchy belly before the paramedics could even find him in the vineyard maze, for the first time in what may have been his whole life, he wished he hadn't really been his father's son after all.

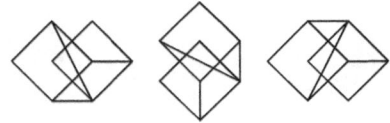

# The Beautifully Framed Mirror

Once upon a time there was a beautifully framed mirror. Not a particularly special mirror in itself, if I'm being frank. Although it might have been once, but mirrors have no memory so it never could tell me. They can only reflect the moment and a snapshot, not a lifetime or a whole story.

That's one of the beautiful things about mirrors.

And at the time of our story, wherever the beautifully framed mirror had been before, now it found itself outside a busy train station toilet, in the walkway where men and women split and go their separate ways. It would be rushed by, and rarely loitered at, reflecting stressed faces or backs of heads as people walked away, shaking their hands and breaking into a little run to make it to their platform. It was a walkway, walk-by kind of mirror, with a walk-away-fast kind of view.

The beautifully framed mirror had been there for years. At least it felt like it had, because sometimes it would feel a ripple of a face it had perhaps seen before and somehow felt was familiar. Or a person might hold their own gaze a second longer than their usual swoosh past, and the mirror would wonder, 'Are they talking to me?' But the feeling would pass as fast as the next face filled its frame. And then a child would call for its mother and the mirror would wish it could angle itself down and see the little ones that it often heard but rarely saw, unless a daddy happened to carry one on his shoulders and then they were usually giggling and happy and sometimes even waving right into the mirror's heart.

So the mirror was fixed, and its passers by were fast. But at one time on some special day when the antique glass roof of the train station was clean enough and a cloud-free sky allowed it, the beautifully framed mirror flashed a ray of sunlight right into the eyes that usually, all too briefly, glazed over its surface. And that light was so blinding, so bright, that it could even stop a train. Because it was a strange light that let the passer by who was passing by so split second fast, just very briefly glimpse themselves as they truly could be: beautiful beyond the silly standards of this world. And more than once when this happened, there were madcap, comic, crazy collisions in the walkway as someone's split-second-shocked stumble started off a sort of domino effect which shuddered its way back to Platform 2, and so made the train for Charing Cross sometimes up to seven minutes late.

Now our beautifully framed mirror got quite good at its little sunlight trick. If a mirror could laugh it would have chuckled with delight when it learnt that it could send out this breathtaking secondary sunlight. It would bounce off a business man's glinting spectacles, or a lady's locket, or sometimes even off the train window as it pulled into the station. It learnt to summon up a rainbow in a nanosecond that it would then catch and reflect straight out onto an unsuspecting passer by. The mirror liked to pick passers by who looked as if they were just coming down with a cold, or had broken up with their boyfriend, or were wearing extremely painful shoes. And always, they would stop, just for a heartbeat, and hang awestruck in that glowing reflection, asking themselves 'Is that really me?!' The mirror would will itself to whisper back, 'Yes...do you see how beautiful you truly are?!'

But it knew it never could, as another very wonderful quality of mirrors is that they cannot speak – which is almost as wonderful as their lack of memory.

So in less than a moment, these golden moments were gone, and the station master's whistle or the chatter of the Albanian cleaning lady would jolt the mirror back to its long waiting game, waiting for a time when the sun might break through to be bounced out for others to bathe in for a very precious heartbeat again.

At the time we spoke, winter was coming. And the mirror had a strange feeling that when the passers by covered themselves with more clothes, it somehow had less chance to bounce the light into the eyes of those rushing past. The time felt suddenly darker, and a sense of foreboding started to crackle in its crystals, as hats and scarves and gloves piled on to its passers by. Each layer felt a sign in itself that the fun was over for another year.

Or maybe, just maybe, the beautifully framed mirror had heard that there was going to be a refurbishment of the old station and that the entrance to the toilets would be moved from just next to the florists, as it had never felt quite right, and the mirror's walkway was to become the back wall of a takeaway donut machine. But let's not be silly, because mirrors can't work out such clever plans, can they?

The best that can be said is it just didn't feel as bright. The sunlight wasn't easy to capture, and the bouncing slipped into that vague memory place too.

*Did I do something sparkling once?* the mirror was asking itself, as one day a man with a tape measure paced the walkway and stopped, not even to look properly into the mirror, but to pick at the flaking edges of its beautiful frame and try to jiggle it about on its fixings. His glasses were square, black framed without even a hint of a glint, and his eye was too busy spotting the florist's deep cleavage bouncing in the corner of the mirror to change his focus and really see his own reflection.

*Why bother anymore?* the mirror thought to itself, feeling an overwhelming sense of foreboding and hopelessness, and that soon an eternal view of a bland storage cupboard wall was its fate, or worse, that it might be shattered into a jagged senseless, disjointed jigsaw at the bottom of a skip.

But behind the black glasses man, a girl was standing, some way off, not rushing anywhere. *Maybe she's thinking about buying flowers for a friend, the mirror thought. But why is she looking at me? Is someone finally speaking to me?* But the mirror suspected that somehow the girl had bounced her spirit into its frame and that's why this winter now felt the darkest ever. The girl just looked and looked as everyone else rushed by and only glimpsed. She gazed blankly, as if she could see right through the mirror, see through the wall, see through her own reflection. But the mirror had nothing to give her, no chink of light, nothing to sparkle, no hope of a rainbow in this overcast old place. 'You're beautiful!' it tried to cry, but knew she neither heard nor saw it, although she eerily continued to look and stare and gaze.

And then the girl turned. She walked slowly, which itself stood out like a screaming shaft of light in the darkness. Then she decisively came to a stop, right on the edge of the platform with her toes reaching, finding and creeping over the very kerb, as the crowds jostled and shuffled and bustled for their train around her.

At that moment, the man with the black framed glasses jiggled the mirror forcibly in frustration one last time, and the florist caught the line of his leering eye and suddenly stopped bending over the hydrangeas she was arranging and stood upright very sharply, deliberately removing the unintended invitation to the man's imagination.

The diamond heart her husband had bought her swung and spun in defiance at her neckline, almost in slow motion according to the mirror, and she fingered it instinctively, protectively, like her talisman, to make her feel less like a piece of meat than the man with black glasses was making her feel.

That diamond, with a power all of its own, glinted a glorious shaft of rainbow light, just enough for the beautifully framed mirror to catch and bounce off, way far out with all its might, straight to Platform 2 where the girl's eye was caught by it falling at her dangerously balanced feet at the very split second she was about to give in and let go of her balance in front of the 10.23 from Oxford.

And at that moment a passer by happened to nudge her with a 'Careful Luv', so that both her feet took two small but critical steps backwards just as the train rushed on by.

At least, that's how the mirror thought it remembered it. And that's the scene that it played in its beautiful frame from that day. Over and over it played it, in secret delight behind the donut vending machine. Because for some reason, its fixings had turned out to be far too tight to shift without shattering the mirror and the man in the black framed glasses turned out to be as superstitious as he was lecherous.

The beautifully framed mirror was delighted, just still to be at the station; because however limited its view, and however small its world, somehow it had found its place.

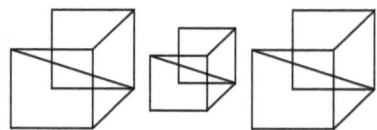

# The Naughty Pair of Lovers

Once upon a time there was a naughty pair of lovers. Now, of course, most lovers have an air of naughtiness about them. You've seen it yourself, when you've looked around a train carriage and spotted glinting cheeky smiles passed between a couple who've been nothing short of contorting and cavorting acrobats only an hour before. Neither them, nor anyone else who spots the glint, can quite believe they're sitting nice and neatly now, only allowing themselves a nervous knee-squeeze, and only occasionally.

The naughtiness I'm talking about is due to the fact that these lovers shouldn't have been together at all. Oh, they were star-crossed and destined and it was impossible that they shouldn't have collided, I will give them that. But his young wife would have split her from lip to lip, as 'she' was old enough to be his mother, and certainly old enough to have known better, to add a knife-twisting insult to their secret wife-threatening injury.

But passion is not picky about circumstance it seems, and so they didn't stand a chance once they had set eyes on each other: over her Calvin Klein bifocals and his Mini Cooper cufflinks in a very boring business meeting, which then suddenly somehow transformed into the opening bars of the most dramatic opera, perhaps maybe ever. Mrs Robinson, in her stockings, grinned at Verdi.

Yes, opera is fitting, as opera is tragic. For theirs was an impossible love; utterly crap young husband that he was, his children would have unrivalled first place in his heart when they came along, and she knew it would be so. And, though aging femme fatale was she, her destiny – which she deep down had known perhaps from aeons gone by, but certainly since her divorce settlement – was to be, ultimately, alone. But until the stuff hit the fan in a big stinking bomb, inevitably they were inseparable; at least in those times that they could both wangle to be so. It was as if they recharged and rebooted, and hoisted each other up overhead to finger heaven's edge and just check that it was still there, before they had to scurry off quickly, wiping lipstick off hastily, to their not-so-merry and now-by-comparison completely hum drum lives.

They liked to meet most of all in the neon-lit Big City, sassy and exciting and full of potential reasons to explain why one of them at least might be there (when they should have been on a conference in a quaint country hotel with a landlady called Janet fussing over her full English and policing any funny business 'he' might get up to with silly young women). Well, far from it.

One night, they were in their bright-lights Big City celebrating some business to do with winning an Olympic contract that might mean gold in her PR pocket – not to mention plenty more opportunities for the naughty pair of lovers to meet up. Bubbles flowed, much chinking followed, and then lengthy acrobatics such that the naughty pair of lovers laid in extremely late by sheer accident for the very first time in their usually militarily precisely run lives.

'I'm so sorry! I'll drive you into the City – it'll be quicker, I know a shortcut,' she said, maternally passionate.

And while he protested that he'd just leg it through Aldgate tube and fend his way, she was wearing that skirt that whilst seemingly demure in length was nearly split to the waist when you understood how it worked, and afforded him far more fun in the passenger seat of her car than standing in a sardine can tube train, even next to a half-naked youthful porn star. He did have some shame. And some love. And, of course, a host of fantasies about a sassy older woman whisking him off in a racing green soft-topped-and-cream leather-seated Jaguar.

'What's all this traffic about? Hang on…what are you doing? You don't need the tunnel…Bollocks, I'll definitely be late now!' his youthful panic blurted.

'Sorry, darling…' she purred. 'I don't know what I was thinking,' she honestly confessed, as she tried to refocus whilst swinging off down Blackwall for some bizarre and unknown reason; but it might have been something to do with the long elegant fingers of his right hand exploring where the top of her left thigh ended and the crease became a crevice, she thought.

Then for the first time that day, because very naughty lovers sometimes disconnect so far from reality that it takes a really concentrated and deliberate effort to come back at all, he removed his hand, and turned on the car radio.

'A second bomb has now exploded and police are advising commuters to evacuate the tube. Do not travel into the City if your journey can be avoided.'

But, as this was a meeting that could make or break his about-to-bloom career, the naughty pair of lovers carried on. They had a habit of doing that. Who knows what their real motives were. In growing terror they crawled past the bleeding wounded, who were fleeing and reeling from stations. Then she had to sit in a car clouded with choking panic and frantic Russian roulette feelings, while he tried to secure a jackpot apprenticeship in the best consultancy house in the world.

Then they both finally saw sense (because sometimes they did) and they tried to beat a hasty retreat. But it would take them nearly seven hours to get safely away from the flashing lights and sirens of the Big City and then very many years to forget...if they ever did.

Jammed fast as the filling between a sandwich of two terror-filled red buses with nowhere to go in forward or reverse gear, they heard the radio announcer gravely report that the Number 30 bus at Tavistock Square had just exploded.

He squeezed her hand tighter – he hadn't loosened his grip one inch since he'd got back to the car after a meeting he now couldn't even remember, and didn't even care to.

'I'm glad I'm with you,' he said and looked deep into her welling up eyes.

She forced a smile and felt sure she was about to say that she couldn't quite believe they were sitting here neatly like ducks on a fairground target waiting for their fate, only nervously knee-squeezing, and only occasionally...

When the next big stinking bomb went off.

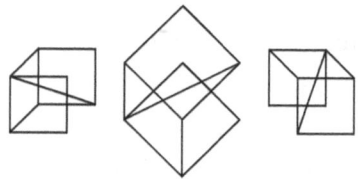

# The Dirty Little Habit

Once upon a time there was a dirty little habit. And this dirty little habit was extremely clever, because whatever form it took, and it could be as varied as the myriad shapes that clouds can shift to, yet forever it remained utterly universal. Yes, everyone, everywhere, had a small piece of it, hidden away, somewhere. And so the dirty little habit spent its life smirking in contentment that at some point in everyone's life, it would have its way.

It didn't mind how it manifested. Whether it was someone who forgot themselves in public and let their finger drift down from way up their left nostril to between their teeth, or someone who couldn't help cruising images that became were more perverse daily to get the kick they needed, or even someone else who was on their second box of cookies before lunch, it really didn't mind.

Best of all it liked to make mischief with those who professed, or especially with those who had a profession, that demanded it was denied out of all existence. It gloried in the lengths that those in vestments or caged-within moral codes – yes and even good mothers – would go to in order to dabble secretly in its delights. Some of those lengths looked rather painful, and frankly quite bizarre, and required a degree of planning worthy of a government intelligence agency. It quite liked that too.

It also rather liked it when some poor, lost individual who'd dumped it years ago, came back, grovelling and professing love and saying how much it had missed it in the barren years. Many a first puff on a cigarette after several smoke-free years had it whooping in delight. Normally this was drowned out by a relieved gasp or groan by the poor lost lamb who had just ambled back into the wolf's fold thinking it an oasis. But sometimes you could just hear a slow hand clap if you listened outside late night bars or in Accident & Emergency car parks.

Yes, it knew that it was irresistible. Not in a devilish sort of way, although it was often portrayed as such in cartoons, with a horned, ruddy face whispering over someone's shoulder. This played right into its hands. It was irresistible because in reality it took the form of an angel of mercy, and when someone's distracted, looking to beat the wrong attacker, just a gentle purr can be far more effective than a full-on punch to defeat even the best-constructed defences.

But one day its universal reign was challenged. A flashy TV guy in a white suit with a voice like silk started purring the gospel of mind control for the masses. He was more prolific than any habit: he was like a virus, getting slots on every chat show, his own mini-series and churning out a small library of self-help books on how to get rid of this habit and that. He was nothing short of a modern day guru using the media to peddle his wares, with the winning pitch that he could make you basically snow white clean with just a bit of mental reprogramming. Jesus would have had a fight on his hands.

As realisation gradually dawned, the dirty little habit went into a flat mad panic. Because it knew that whilst some of its hook was linked to various kinds of pleasant chemical rush, its real hold was in individuals' minds. Longing for an angel in a world that ridicules them can make space for all sorts of mental opportunities to elbow into these spaces and abuse them to bits. And a mind guru knew those spaces like the back of his manicured hand, and had pitched his flag every which where, building a common wealth of twentieth-century common man's own neurological strength.

'Enough!' snapped the dirty little habit one day and willed itself to shift its shape right into the TV guru's palatial LA residence, stalking his hallways in a dark cloudy shadow until it came face to face with him for the showdown of its life.

Now earlier that day, the TV guru had lost a loved one: a life angel to him who had propped and soothed and purred in support behind him at every step of his entire empire of a career. And it so happened that on that day the cleaning lady had left a bag of goodies on the kitchen counter top, bought for her beloved husband's sixtieth birthday, including a bottle of his favourite malt whisky. The TV guru had been irresistibly partial to this malt in his time too.

'Go on – you need it; you can replace it by tomorrow, no harm done. No one need ever even know…' the dirty little habit whispered grittily as the TV guru's eyes rested on the bottle.

And the TV guru twisted the cap and took a big swig.

The cock-a hoop-whoop was audible to one so wired, and the TV guru spun around to face the dirty little habit full on, which somehow looked oddly like a circus mirror reflection of the TV guru himself.

'You think you've won, don't you?' the TV guru said.

'Well, that's pretty obvious, isn't it?' smirked the dirty little habit back at him. 'You're a fraud, no more of a guru than any I've ever met, and most of those are now in the gutter, prison or dead,' the dirty little habit laughed. 'Drink up!'

And the TV guru took another big gulp. And then another.

Then he slowly, steadily, opened his bread bin and took out a baguette and broke it in half, and pulled off a small piece and ate it, savouring.

And he turned to the dirty little habit and railed at it and on it to the point that it looked nothing like him anymore but just small and ruddy and horned and seething.

'If I had a cigar, I'd light that too! But for now, this cake candle will do…'

Then the dirty little habit felt itself shrink and drain away in the force of the honour and celebration of remembrance for the best time that the TV guru and his friend had ever shared. The guru reverently performed nothing short of a eulogy Eucharist that reinforced and relived all the radical life-affirming and life-changing things from that night in Paris when they'd talked through their dreams until four in the morning. Each friend had believed in his best friend's mission. It had been utterly mutual.

'What you forget,' the TV guru said, 'is that addiction is not always to destruction. The very strongest hook and hit of all is the power to choose which it will be.'

The dirty little habit, who knew no other way of being, turned tail and slunk off with what was left of itself to stalk another hallway.

Because celebration, apart from of defeat, really wasn't its thing.

Such a shame really; it didn't have a choice.

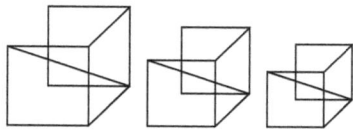

# The Iconic Image

Once upon a time there was an iconic image that totally epitomised sensuality in a way which had never been seen before. That sounds like a bold claim. But, this was an image that men of any age, could not help but dream of once they had seen it, when they allowed themselves to daydream on such things. Which might be every three seconds if research is to be believed. Although more likely it happens when they're stuck for monotonous hours on the motorway, or endlessly sorting the weeds in the garden. But mostly, I do have to tell you, this iconic image came to mind in the bathroom when the door was locked.

You know what I mean...

The iconic image was of a woman whose attraction was beyond just the ratio of her nose to her full, moist lips, although this ratio was certainly perfect. It has to be said, so it is with many women who never make it to a glossy magazine cover or a bus stop advert or a poster adorning millions of adolescent boys' walls. Indeed sometimes a far less than perfect ratio can be far more beautiful.

But it was the iconic image's eyes that connected most with every man who saw her, and plenty of women too I dare say, in a way that was nothing short of bewitching. It was as if her very pupils and irises could whisper beguilingly, 'Fall into me, I'll hold you safely, I'll love you.' It certainly was absolutely nothing to do with cup size or a plastic pout.

So it was a very rare man who couldn't help but respond to this call, often whilst doing something pretty unsafe in their sheds with one eye on the kitchen window where their wife was making marmalade. Or maybe in the five minutes before the kids came clattering home from school, and the man happened to be home alone as he rarely had been since Ben was born seven years ago and Lily came so swiftly after – or at least, he'd probably only been home alone the number of times he could count on his favourite left hand.

You do know what I mean...

You see, the iconic image was so amazingly bewitching that she would pop up, all over the world, in millions of minds, daily. She had a few rivals: there was a snapshot of a tennis player without any knickers on somewhere. But she knew that image was only iconic in the sense that metro signs are universally recognisable and you know if you go down the stairs you'll be on a train to a certain destination. So she wasn't worried.

Because she felt that she was iconic in a way that the Mona Lisa might have been. She'd heard this power discussed once, but then got muddled when an academic woman with severe spectacles – who was using her in a slideshow during a lecture for women somewhere – had said categorically that this 'Lisa' was a man. All things are possible, she supposed. So from then she liked to think that somehow her iconic image was a bit like the Red Cross – a symbol of hope for those who needed rescuing, and a sign that help was on its way.

Well, she hoped as much, at least. That there was real care and the offer of more than just a basic relief in the promise that her bewitching eyes portrayed; and she suspected as much, as oftentimes men would release long held-in tears that they very quickly stashed away as swiftly as any other evidence if they saw their lovely wife unexpectedly pop out of the back door with a mug of tea and a bacon sandwich. And certainly if they heard Ben and Lily rattle and clatter up the drive with their over-laden backpacks far too soon after school.

The key to the iconic image's power, or so she'd overheard two garage mechanics in a pub one day say, was 'once seen, never forgotten'. She liked that. She liked that a lot. And she imagined, by contrast, that the fans of the tennis girl had to actually find the picture and check: 'Oh yes, no panties, white ankle socks' for it to work its charm.

In that sense, the poor tennis girl got hit on in a very basic way far more than the iconic image ever did, and these days you could do that from the privacy of your bedroom as long as you owned a mouse, apparently. And you didn't even have to venture out to a picture or a poster shop.

So the iconic image didn't need to be hit on, because 'once seen, never forgotten'. It had the power to burn a space in the viewer's brain that didn't need a frame or to be kept folded up small in the back of a wallet (just in case), or secreted in a shoebox behind the rusting garden hammock and the scary weedkiller bottle (just to be safe).

*This* was its power. To become a secret part of the viewer forever and, in so doing, help those who felt the need to express part of their secret selves in a way that they otherwise might never manage in the lives they had somehow chosen to lead.

Now, all this knowledge of power can go to an image's, or anything else for that matter's, head. The iconic image was certainly within its rights to come over all Queeny and diva-ish, demanding the right to appear only on Champagne adverts and securing private member-only viewings by millionaires in limousines.

But she didn't. In fact, very far from it. She could laugh at the picture of a stunning film star with her bright white skirts blowing up about her ears as she stood over some air vent. Apparently there was now a star somewhere with her name on it and even presidents had crumbled at her beauty (allegedly).

But this wasn't the desire or dream of the iconic image that we're talking about. It was far less Hollywood and much more concerned about the nervous chap in the dentist's waiting room who needed something to distract him from the sound of the drill he'd been playing in his head for the last two days. And for a while, well at least until the injections in his gum had taken hold, her eyes would whisper to him to drown out the revving

'Fall into me, I'll hold you safely, I'll love you'

And for a while he heard her over a world that suddenly sounded so metal.

Soon after, as she lay atop the pile of magazines he'd left in the waiting room – albeit a bit dog-eared and over-thumbed and with a coupon cut out of her chin – she happened to find herself on top of an image on the back of another magazine which had been created for an aftershave, with nothing short of a buffed up Tarzan draping his torso in perfect sunlight across the stern of a fantasy castaway boat, in his perfect teeny tiny designer pants.

'Oh...it's you!' the buffed up Tarzan image said. 'My God...those eyes...but we're too close...I can't help myself...'

And as with all men, the Tarzan image in the advert at that moment just couldn't help falling into her.

And there he found himself, back in the studio where

the iconic image was being made originally, with a sweaty cigar-smoking director demanding more sex from her, to make love to the camera, to fuck it within an inch of its life.

And the model who was trying so hard to make the iconic image gazed at the Tarzan with eyes as dead as someone who's woken in a concentration camp. She looked like someone who would clearly prefer to be shot instantly than to fight for the hopeless survival plan of using a teaspoon to dig a tunnel that might just get one yard beyond the bloodthirsty dogs and barbed wire perimeter fence. If you were lucky.

'Give me more!' the director bellowed, knowing that with every second he was running over budget.

But the Tarzan watched the model's eyes roam in disillusioned detachment to the cameraman's newspaper. Then they suddenly fixed on an image which had been taken very far away from the swanky London studio of the shoot. It was an image of another country…where a baby girl no bigger than a stray cat had been abandoned on a pavement, and businessmen and schoolchildren rushed by on their morning commutes without ever looking, without ever even seeing the babe left to die like a scavenger rat, perhaps fearing it might give them the plague if they admitted that such a thing lurked in their society.

But the model's eyes saw it. The model who had no hope of her own babies as she'd had to purge herself of one when not much more than one herself and so, by fate's cruel twist, screwed up her chances forever. And she only met director types now who wanted her to bear their needs and lives and no one else's.

'That's it!' cried the director, 'That's the look I want!' nearly swallowing his cigar in excitement.

And the hot and heaving cameras shot at her like a blaze of gunfire, a burst of paparazzi frenzy, to capture something that so far all their technical tricks with lighting and makeup and image manipulation had not achieved.

At this very second the Tarzan was pulled back to his advert, because a stylish young woman who was in for a whitening treatment was reaching for him and wondering what to get for her lover for Christmas. And Tarzan had a job to do.

But as he drifted away from the shoot, back to the dentist's waiting room, back to his castaway boat he clearly heard the iconic image's eyes say to the other unforgettable iconic image they had locked onto:

'Fall into me, I'll hold you safely, I'll love you'.

And he knew, without a doubt, that he'd never ever forget her.

Much like everyone else.

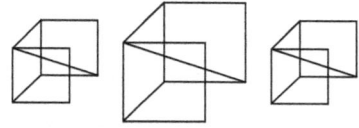

# The Stick of Cherry Red Chalk

Once upon a time there was a stick of cherry red chalk. It was the kind of shade that you would squeal about finding in a pack, so rich and vibrant that you could eat it. Well, if you're into those kinds of things I guess. Enough to say, it was the double yolk equivalent in the chalk world – a little treasure tucked away quietly in its box. A kid's oyster wrapped in a cardboard shell.

Now...I'll let you into a secret: sticks of chalk only come alive when they are being used. Back in the box, or basically whenever they're not in someone's fingers, they're as fast asleep as a baby breast-fed with milk laced with brandy.

It's a wonderful state.

But of course, it means that each moment they're awoken feels a rather rude wake-up call. Like a bucket of ice water thrown in your face followed by a jab in the eye with a red hot poker. Or electric paddles in an emergency ward.

Or all three.

To prove my point, the first time the stick of cherry red chalk was woken it was being whizzed across a blackboard with lightening speed and a mid-air frenzy, underlining and highlighting and squiggling crazy-shaped stars that gave it a blinding, shocking headache, given the passion that the lecturer clearly had for his subject. It was a rollercoaster birth and it had to get its head in gear pretty quickly.

As it did, it worked out that it was being used in a lecture on culture, pulling themes of philosophy and science and all sorts of artistic endeavours together in a great big blackboard clock face, which started with the ancient world at about one o'clock and ticked right on round to the twenty-first century chiming in at midnight.

The stick of cherry red chalk quickly worked out that it was definitely getting all the good bits. It was liberally scrawled all over the renaissance, had a total hoot dancing around Da Vinci, and 'Digital Age' even got written in red alone so that it shone out like a beacon. So bright it was that it blasted right out across the lecture hall and into the brain of a student who had never even thought about these things. Certainly not in quite that way. Her neural pathways were suddenly ignited and sparked by that trail of red chalk dust in a manner that would make her potentially even greater than Da Vinci, as it was to turn out. Yes, the inspired, creative story of her life would start straight after that lecture, in the time it took for a large cappuccino and a call to her uncle about funding a trip to Rome.

But when the bell rang the stick of cherry red chalk was put back in its box.

The next time it was woken it seemed to be at a bus stop somewhere and it could smell burning. It was being twiddled and scribbled in a random doodle while a girl with a lot of metal in her face also twiddled and sucked on a white smoking stick in her other hand. She seemed to like both her sticks just about equally. And as she jangled on her way home she used nearly all that was left of the stick of cherry red chalk to graffiti quirky little messages on walls and ledges and even on pavements, like 'Enjoy your day' and 'Let yourself shine'.

And because it didn't rain for a few days, this trail the stick of cherry red chalk left raised endless smiles and hopes and even a sense of the beyond in a few of those who read the seemingly out of context words and then couldn't forget them on the morning bus to a job they hated –

Not until the next downpour anyway.

The very last time the stick of cherry red chalk was woken was by some fat stubby sticky baby fingers that didn't grab at it with any of the skill of its other two owners. In fact, at one point it was fumbled off the coffee table and pawed and toyed with by something that surely couldn't have been human, with nails like vicious little knives and a tongue made of wet fishy sandpaper. It heard distant shouting, and the pawing monster suddenly scarpered with a tail swish that happened to roll it back into the chubby grubby fingers, which didn't want to let the stick of cherry red chalk go back to sleep...not just yet...

So it was swooped up, copying the kitty cat, and the stick of cherry red chalk was licked and sucked to within an inch of its life – as it was now so small it looked a bit like a cherry red sweetie anyway.

And what was left of the stick of cherry red chalk finally came to rest in the throat of the child with an innocent sweet tooth, nestling down snugly in her windpipe and neatly shutting out the draughty air supply so that both of them could sleep soundly, deep and dreamily.

And who would want to wake up from that kind of wondrous sleep anyway?

During those eternal slumbers, neither the child nor the stick of cherry red chalk knew anything of the frenzy of mass TV coverage, and children's charity campaigns and phone-in shows on parental neglect that followed. Nor did they know of the new safer homes the poor child's numerous brothers and sisters were swiftly shifted off to by social workers, in the hope that they could create their lives to the full, enjoy all their days, and have their chance to blaze a trail.

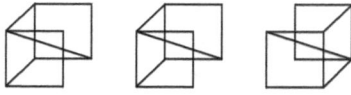

*Storytellers broaden our minds: engage, provoke,*
*inspire and ultimately connect us*

Robert Redford

www.ingramcontent.com/pod-product-compliance
Lightning Source LLC
Chambersburg PA
CBHW050903180626
46814CB00007B/2881